Princess Time

The Princess and the Pea

Miles Kelly

Once upon a time, there was a handsome prince. He had everything he could wish for, but was quite lonely.

His parents, the king and queen, said that it might be time for him to look for a bride.

The prince thought this was a good idea, so he started his search for the perfect princess.

He held parties all over the kingdom, where he met plenty of perfectly pleasant girls who **said they were princesses.**

He also met some unpleasant princesses.
None, it seemed to him, were quite right.

But he carried
on looking...

The prince travelled to faraway lands, where royal families presented a host of suitable young ladies.

But there was always something not quite right – such as too many pets...

...or terrible table manners! Nowhere could he find a princess who lived up to his

high standards.

So the prince returned to his palace, where he sat reading dusty books and getting **very glum.**

One wintery night, there was the most terrible storm. The prince huddled close to the fire.

Just as everyone was going to bed there was a loud knocking at the door. The king, queen and prince went to see who it was.

Knock, knock!

There, absolutely dripping wet and covered in mud, stood a girl.

No one could have looked less like a princess, but that is exactly what the girl claimed to be.

Everyone thought it was very unlikely that the girl was a princess, but they invited her in and told her to take a seat by the fire.

The girl sat sipping a mug of warm milk and slowly dried off.

As the girl grew warmer the prince noticed how rosy her cheeks were, and how pretty her laugh.

Woof Woof!

The queen noticed the attention her son was paying to this mystery girl, and she decided to test whether or not she really was a princess.

The queen went to the finest spare bedroom, and gave orders to the maids.

She told them to take
all of the bedclothes
and the mattress
off the bed.

Then she placed
one single pea
on the middle of
the bedstead.

Next the maids piled dozens of mattresses, sheets, feather quilts and warm blankets on top of the pea.

Then the girl was shown
to her room and left
alone for the night.

In the morning, the queen swept into the bedroom and asked the girl,

"How did you sleep, your highness?"

"I didn't sleep a wink all night," she replied. "There was a great, hard lump in the middle of the bed. It was quite dreadful. I am sure I am black and blue all over!"

The queen was delighted. This meant that the girl really was a princess, for only a true princess could be as sensitive as that.

"She is a princess, after all!"

The prince proposed to the princess at once,
and they lived happily ever after.

The pea was placed in the royal museum, where it probably still is today.

THE PEA